# A SHADOW HEART

HE IS HER CAPTOR...
AND HER ONLY SALVATION

AND OTHER DARK LOVE STORIES

## SHIRLEY SIATON

ISBN 978-1-961052-66-6 (paperback, *romance*)
ISBN 978-621-8431-19-5 (paperback, *discreet*)

*1st Edition, September 2025*

Published by Inky Sword Book Publishing
Romance cover design by Angeline Cantila
Discreet cover design by Marika Veil
Interior formatting by Champagne Book Design

**Inky Sword Book Publishing**
Barangay Quezon, Arevalo, Iloilo City 5000
Republic of the Philippines
inkysword.com

# A NOTE FOR THE READER

The love stories you are about to read live in the twilight. They are about the bonds that form in the dark, the beauty found in broken things, and the profound, often painful marks that people leave on one another.

These are not gentle tales. They are intense, emotional, and intended for a mature audience.

To ensure you can navigate these pages with care, please be aware that this collection includes:

- Explicit sexual content
- High-stakes situations, including kidnapping and violence
- Discussions of past physical abuse and trauma
- Portrayals of toxic relationship dynamics
- Characters grappling with self-destructive behaviors
- Heavy angst and emotionally raw themes

Thank you for choosing to explore this world of shadow hearts and bruise-colored love. Please read kindly and look after yourself.

To all my readers

Thank you for two wonderful years of dark love stories

Here's to a hundred more

# CONTENTS

# A
# SHADOW
# HEART

# CHAPTER 1

## The Lights

**T**HE LIGHTS ARE TOO BRIGHT.

Not the kind I'm used to—neon signs flickering in seedy motels, or the sterile glow of Makati towers.

These are cheap, borrowed bulbs strung across bamboo poles, their wires sagging, their glow uneven. But it works. The coffee shop looks alive.

Music spills out into the street, a mix of OPM classics and whatever upbeat trash the DJ they hired could cobble together. The banner above the little shop reads *Brew & Break: Coffee for the Puyat Generation.*

It's all clever. And true.

I know I shouldn't be here, but I am.

The job offer hasn't come in yet. No contract. No instructions.

I'm only here to watch. To learn. That's what I tell myself. But my eyes keep finding her.

Lara Bienvenides. A politician's daughter. A Congressman's pretty little gem. She shouldn't normally be anywhere near this crowd. The coffee shop is filled with a mix of students in uniforms, call center kids still in ID lanyards, and yuppies clutching cheap plastic tumblers like trophies.

But here she is, with her older brother Luke. He owns the place and she works for him. It's not a secret that they have left their parents to strike out on their own. Their father, Lawrence, had been implicated one too many times in misspent pork barrel investigations and disappearing flood control projects, but he's slipped out all of them fairly unscathed.

Lara has the sleeves of her simple white shirt rolled up. Her hair's tied back, a few strands sticking to her forehead with sweat. She's carrying trays of iced coffee and complimentary cookies, laughing with strangers, brushing errant sugar and crumbs off her jeans as moves around the room.

She looks free.

And it makes something twist in my chest.

A group of young men and women invite me to join their table, but I ignore them. I'm leaning against the far wall, shadowed, my usual place wherever I am. I sip the cold bottle of light beer I bought just to blend in.

My mask is off. Not the cloth one, but the mask of distance. Tonight, I let myself watch.

Later, Luke makes a speech. It's nervous and awkward, about dreams and hard work and no shortcuts. The crowd cheers him on. Lara claps the loudest. Her smile is proud, fond, and real.

It doesn't take long before couples take to the tiny space in the middle of the shop, set up as a makeshift dance floor.

Then the music changes to something slow, almost moody. An old Rivermaya song, maybe.

Before I know what I'm doing, I push off the wall.

Lara's near the counter, wiping away sweat from her forehead with a white handkerchief, a small smile of relief on her delicate face. She looks up, startled, when I stop in front of her.

My voice comes out low and steady. Not a request. Not quite a command.

"Dance with me."

# CHAPTER 2

## The Dance

"**D**ANCE WITH ME."

The words cut through the noise of the crowd. Not loud or demanding. Just steady, like he knew I'd hear him.

I look up, startled, wiping sweat from my forehead with my handkerchief.

He's a stranger, distinctly taller than most people in the room. He's broad-shouldered, hair swept back from his face and tied neatly, face too angular and sharp-featured to be handsome. A scar cuts across his left cheek.

He's dressed too plainly to be one of Kuya's investors, too clean to be one of the neighborhood kids, too casual to be working at one of the offices nearby. It's just a plain black shirt over some dark jeans.

I should laugh, tell him no. But something in his dark eyes holds me still. Something deep and unspoken. I feel like they've been on me all night.

And maybe I like that.

So I nod.

His hand closes around mine. It's large and calloused, his grip warm and certain. My pulse jumps.

He draws me into the open space where couples sway to Rivermaya. His other hand settles at my waist, steady, anchoring me in the crush of the crowd.

My body tenses, then softens as he guides me. He's close, close enough that I can feel the heat of him through my sweaty shirt, close enough that his chest brushes mine when we change tempo or angles.

"What's your name?" I ask, because I need words to distract myself from how hard my heart is beating.

"Jace." His voice is deep, slightly raspy at the edges. I imagine it whispering my name, and heat rushes to my face.

"Jace…" I repeat, trying it out. It fits. Strong, short, and dangerous. "I'm Lara."

"I know." His mouth almost curves, like he's smiling at some private joke.

He doesn't smell like anyone else here—not beer, not sweat, not even cologne. Just rain and smoke and something clean that clings to my skin when I breathe him in.

"You don't look like someone who hangs out at coffee shop launches," I murmur.

"First time." His gaze never leaves mine. "Worth it."

"Well, that's nice to hear," I say. "You should visit more often. Support local businesses."

"Maybe I should," he answers softly. "If I get to see you like this."

I blush again, swallowing as I look away.

He doesn't say anything, but his hand on my waist digs a little deeper into the fabric of my shirt, the heat seeping into my skin underneath.

The song is ending.

I don't want it to.

He leans in, close enough that his breath brushes my ear. "Thank you for the dance. Goodnight, Lara."

And then he's gone.

He just lets me go, as if the moment never mattered, and disappears into the night.

I stand frozen in the middle of the crowd, breathless, my skin tingling where he touched it, my heart still racing like I've just stepped off the rooftop of a skyscraper.

Whatever the hell that was…

I'm not walking away from it unchanged.

# CHAPTER 3

**T**HE BAR SMELLS OF STALE GIN AND WET ASHTRAYS. I don't remember how many times I've been here before, but I know it's always to pick up my end of a contract. My handler likes the place because no one really asks too many questions.

I sit in the corner booth, shadowed and waiting. The woman arrives late—sharp cream suit, a sharper humorless smile, the kind that says she's paid to make problems vanish. She slides a folder across the table without bothering with pleasantries. This will be my third job with their party.

"Jace," she says, voice smooth. "This one's important. A Congressman's daughter. Leverage. Let's just say we want the old man to get off his high horse."

I don't touch the folder yet. I just listen.

"The girl's visible. Loved by the press. Always on her brother's arm at these little…projects of his. They're trying to build a business empire together, coffee shops and restaurants. A cheap concept, but it makes them accessible, relatable. People like them. Her more so. She's not the usual spoiled rich girl who posts pictures of expensive vacations on social media. She's a college student. All that."

I nod, not saying anything. Politicians don't want their kids to be liked. They want them to be untouchable, just like them. For when the time comes.

"The job is clean," she continues. "Grab her. Hold her. We'll take care of the rest. Price is double your previous fee. We don't want anyone to see or suspect anything. So we got the best in the business for this sort of thing."

I flip the folder open. Photos slide out.

Lara Bienvenides. Up close, in profile, laughing with her brother in front of a coffee cart at Glorietta. Another shot, her in a light dress at some ribbon-cutting event. She looks a bit younger in it.

But it's the same angel of a woman from the party.

Her eyes are just as I remember. Wide, bright, and alive.

I shut the folder before the woman sees too much in my face.

"I'll do it," I say.

"Fifty percent will be wired within the hour," she confirms.

"Make it sixty. I'll let you know when it's time for pick-up." My voice doesn't falter, though my chest feels tight.

She looks at me for a moment, then nods.

"Fine. We'll wait for your call."

In daylight, the coffee shop is small, squeezed between a pawnshop and a convenience store, its new signboard still smelling of paint. Inside, the tables are crowded with students and call center kids nursing cups of cheap caffeine like it's holy water.

I step up to the counter. The menu is handwritten on kraft paper. *Matapang Brew, Puyat Latte, 2AM Americano.*

And then I see her.

She's behind the counter, apron tied around her waist, sleeves rolled up like before. Her thick black hair is in a loose pile at the top of her head. Her skin looks dewy in the soft lights of the shop.

Her brother is in the back arguing with a supplier, and she's running the register herself.

She glances up, and the moment her eyes lock on mine, something clicks into place. Recognition. And wariness. Maybe something else.

For a heartbeat, neither of us speaks.

Then I clear my throat. "Black coffee, please."

She blinks, nods quickly, and turns to pour. The small act—her fingers steady, her hair falling into her face, the steam curling between us—feels louder than the busy chatter of the whole shop.

When she sets the paper cup down between us, our hands almost touch.

"You came back," she says softly.

I wrap my hand around the cup, holding onto the heat. "I said I would. Worth it."

Her lips part, and I see the faintest trace of a smile before she catches herself and looks away.

I turn away without another word, the coffee burning down my throat as I drink it to hide my face.

For the first time in years, the contract feels heavier than the gun under my shirt.

# CHAPTER 4

## The Walk

THE SHOP IS BUSY FOR ANOTHER HOUR OR SO—students bent over their laptops, workers laughing too loudly over greasy plates of fries and sliders, young couples huddled next to each other sharing brownies and carrot cake.

They're the kind of people my brother says we're here for. Affordable coffee and food, decent Wi-Fi, and no one kicking you out if you sit too long.

By the end of my shift, I'm tired. I take off my apron as I say goodbye to the baristas coming in for the night shift. I grab my bag and phone, notebook tucked under my arm for quick reviews during breaks.

I push open the side door, and stop.

He's there.

Jace leans against the lamppost outside the staff entrance, one hand shoved into his jeans pocket, the other loose at his side.

"Hi," I say, a little awkwardly, throat tight. "Waiting for someone?"

"For you," he says simply, as if it explains everything.

I stare at him. "Why?"

"It's late," he says. "I'll walk you wherever you need to go. Or wait until you get a ride."

Something in me wants to argue, to say I can look after myself, to ask what kind of man waits outside a coffee shop for a girl he barely knows. Besides, I know how to handle myself. My father had made sure of that, since Luke and I were kids.

But the truth is, his presence doesn't feel wrong. It feels…protective. Maybe he's already claimed a right to be here, without me knowing.

"I don't need a ride," I tell him as we fall into step together. "I live just a few blocks away. Small apartment. Right next to my brother's. He makes sure I stay in school even with the business. I've got an exam tomorrow."

"You still study?" His gaze flicks to my face curiously.

"Of course I do. Accountancy, actually. I'm not letting Luke carry everything on his back." I hug the notebook tighter to my chest. "He's building something. And I want to be part of it, properly, as a partner in the business. What about you?"

He shrugs. "Computers. A little bit of this and that. Mostly contracts. Never got to finish college, but I get by. I live a few blocks out."

I sneak glances at him. The way the streetlamp hits the sharp lines of his face. The scar half-hidden in the shadows. The way he carries himself—graceful yet quiet, every movement measured.

I can't even tell how old he is. He could easily be twenty-five or forty-five.

Jace doesn't say much as we make our way through the streets, but he doesn't need to. He walks close, his stride steady, like he's watching every shadow we pass.

He's not like anyone I know. He's not like anyone I should ever get close to.

And still, something in me wants to.

We stop at my gate. I should thank him, say goodnight, and go inside.

But instead, I look up at him and the words tumble out on their own. "You didn't have to walk me home."

"I did," he replies, the same way he did earlier.

I don't think.

I put a hand on his shoulder, to make him lean down. Then I rise on my toes and press my lips softly to his. Hesitant but quick, before my courage vanishes.

His breath catches, and I feel the smallest tension in him, as if he might pull me back in for more.

But he doesn't. He lets me have this one reckless choice.

I step away, cheeks hot, heart thundering. "Goodnight, Jace."

I slip inside the building, heart still racing, but I can't quite let it end. The kiss still burns on my lips. The warmth of him still clings to my skin.

So I walk to the small window by my desk and push the curtain aside.

He's still there.

Standing under the lamplight, shoulders squared like he belongs to the night itself. He doesn't move. Then, as if feeling my eyes on him, he looks up straight at my window, and catches me watching.

Heat floods my face and neck. But instead of hiding, I lift my hand and give him a wave.

For a moment, nothing. Then he raises his hand in return. Not playful, not shy—but steady, sure, a silent pact I know but don't understand.

It makes me smile anyway. My chest feels too full, like something new is blooming there, fragile but real.

I lower my hand, letting the curtain fall back into place.

On the street below, I know he's still standing there, still looking.

And I stand in my quiet little room, smiling into the shadows, already falling.

# CHAPTER 5

## The Night

I STAY UNTIL HER SHIFT ENDS.

I listen to the hum of the espresso machine, the sound of chairs scraping against tiles, and the voices of the students and call center kids as they drift out into the night. And still I sit, nursing a coffee gone cold, just to watch her.

Lara moves from table to table, clearing cups and plates. She hums under her breath, absentminded, something soft and tuneless.

She shouldn't be here, in this world where shadows like mine exist. She should belong to the light, where humming and laughter mean something.

Finally, she looks up and sees me still sitting there. Her eyes widen a little. "Jace. You're still here?"

I shrug. "Needed to see how you survived."

Her smile blooms instantly. The sight feels like a full round shot into my chest.

"The exams? Brutal. But I think I passed. Numbers never liked me, but I'm patient with them. Something's gonna give eventually, right?"

"Passing's enough." I lean forward, elbows on the table. "Your brother will be proud."

She tilts her head, studying me like she doesn't quite understand me. "You actually remembered I had exams."

"Of course I did."

Something flickers in her eyes. As if she's not used to people noticing, not like this. She tucks a strand of hair behind her ear, looking flustered, and murmurs, "Most people don't pay attention like that."

I try to smile. As best as I could. "I'm not most people."

She smiles back a little. "No. You're not."

She looks at me for a few more moments before she turns away to finish cleaning up. I watch her pull out her white handkerchief from her pocket and use it to pat away the beads of sweat clinging to her slender neck.

I have never seen something so innocent, yet so erotic.

*Fuck it all.*

I should leave. I should end it here. But instead, I wait for her to finish up, then walk beside her into the night.

The streets are quiet, pools of yellow light stretching under the lampposts. A stray dog barks, a tricycle rattles past.

When she looks at me, her eyes are tired, but soft, almost gentle.

"You don't have to keep walking me home, Jace. I'm used to this neighborhood."

"I know."

"Then why?"

"Because it's late." I glance at her, voice low. "And I'd rather it be me here than someone else."

She slows, just a fraction, as if the words caught her off guard. "You make it sound like the streets are dangerous."

"They are," I say simply.

She studies me, her eyes trying to see beneath the shadows I wear.

"Not when you're around," she replies.

Silence stretches between us. Every step toward her building feels like another step toward the edge of a cliff I can't stop myself from walking off.

At her gate, she stops, turning to me. The lamplight paints her in gold.

She's nervous. I can see it in the way her fingers tighten on the straps of her bag, in the way her breath catches, but she doesn't look away.

"Jace…" Her voice is barely above a whisper. "You're… very different."

I don't ask what she means. I don't want to hear it.

And then she pulls me down by the shirt and kisses me.

It's soft and tentative at first, but it lingers, her hand

brushing lightly against my chest. I feel her heart pounding as fast as mine. When she pulls back, her eyes are shining.

"You're a good man," she says softly.

The words cut through me, raw and merciless. I want to tell her the truth, that I'm anything but, that I'm the danger she doesn't see.

But my voice betrays me. "Don't say that."

"Why not?" she asks gently, almost smiling. "It's true. You look out for me. You don't even realize it, but you do."

Then she reaches up, her fingers lightly tracing over the scar on my cheek.

"You're very special," she says.

I can't breathe.

*She doesn't know.*

Her hand grazes mine as she lowers it and steps back toward her gate. "Goodnight, Jace."

And just like that, she's gone, door closing softly behind her, leaving me outside with my shadows and her words seared into my chest.

*You're a good man. You're very special.*

Just like the night before, I look up to see her standing by the window. She waves to me, a smile on her face.

I wave back.

Then I watch her draw the curtains. I don't move.

I stand there long after the lights in her apartment go dark.

And for the first time in years, I hate myself for the job I already agreed to.

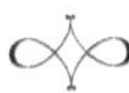

I tell myself not to come.

I tell myself to let her walk home alone tonight, to break the pattern before it becomes something I can't undo.

But I'm here anyway, across the street from where I can see her.

Inside the coffee shop, I see her moving, wiping down a table as she talks to the men coming in for the new shift, stretching her arms like she's already half-asleep.

She's humming again. She doesn't know I hear her through glass, that I carry the sound with me into my dreams.

My chest aches. She waved at me. Smiled at me like I was hers to trust. And today, for hours, I thought about that smile. About her lips pressing to mine at the gate, soft and certain, calling me a good man, telling me I'm someone special.

I almost believed her.

Almost.

Then I remembered the file waiting in my room. Her photo clipped to the top. The promise I made to the woman who pays me to finish this.

And the truth—that nothing about me is good.

The side entrance door opens. Lara steps out, bag slung across her body. She pauses for a moment, glancing down the street.

She's looking for me. I see it in the way her eyes linger on the shadows, the faint crease of disappointment when she thinks I'm not there.

*God.* She wanted me here.

She starts walking. Her footsteps echo against the quiet pavement. I fall into step behind her, silent as I've been trained to be, my body a shadow among shadows.

Three blocks. Then two. My throat is dry.

I should let her go. I should vanish into the dark and forget her name.

I should let the job go.

But my feet move faster.

"Jace?" Her voice is uncertain when I finally step into the spill of the streetlight. She's not afraid. Not yet. She even smiles, faint and relieved. "I thought you weren't coming tonight."

My stomach twists. She doesn't know. She never saw the predator standing in the place of her protector.

I don't answer. I can't. I just reach into my pocket, feel the pouch of dust warm against my palm.

Her smile falters. "What's wrong?"

I step closer. Too close. The scent of coffee and her own cologne clings to her, now dangerously familiar.

"I'm sorry, Lara," I say. "Forgive me."

She opens her mouth to speak, but then I break the pouch, golden powder spilling into the night air.

She gasps, tries to push past me, but her body falters. "Jace…what are you—"

I catch her before she hits the ground. Her head falls against my chest, her lashes fluttering once before the darkness takes her.

I hold her tighter than I should. Too tight for someone who's only a job.

My heart slams against my ribs. She weighs nothing, but carrying her feels like bearing the whole world.

*You're very special.*

Her words echo in my skull.

*You're a good man.*

No. I'm not.

I lift her into my arms and disappear into the waiting shadows.

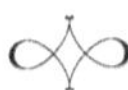

The water scalds my skin, but it isn't enough.

I turn the knob hotter, let it burn across my scar, down my chest, over the hands that carried her here. The sting is better than the cold inside me. Better than thinking about the way she said my name before the darkness closed around her.

Steam fills the bathroom, but it doesn't scrub me clean. The powder dust still clings to my conscience. The lie still rings in my ears.

*You're very special. You're a good man.*

I press my forehead to the tiles and breathe hard. If she knew who hired me, if she knew why, she'd spit at me, claw at me, even fight until she bled.

And yet she smiled at me. She kissed me. She waved from her window.

She believed in a man who never existed.

I twist the knobs off and step out, water trailing down my back, pooling on the tiles. I dry myself quickly, pull on a black shirt and joggers.

No mask now. No gun. Just me. The man in the shadows.

When I open the bathroom door, the room is hushed except for the low hum of the air-conditioner.

She's still asleep.

Lara lies curled on the bed, small beneath the weight of the hotel blanket, her long hair loose and spilled across the pillow. Her breathing is steady, lips parted slightly, face softened into something that feels too pure for the world she's been dragged into.

For a moment, I just stand there. Watching her. Listening to her breathe.

She looks peaceful.

I hate myself for knowing that peace will shatter in a few hours, when I take her to the rooftop. When the client arrives at dawn.

I drag a chair to the far side of the bed, lower myself onto it. My arms rest heavy on my knees, fingers knotting together as if they could hold me in place.

It should be easy. A job's a job. I've done worse.

But I can't stop staring at her. At the girl who called me good. At the girl who kissed me twice, and meant it.

Dawn is coming.

And I don't know if I have the strength to hand her over.

# CHAPTER 6

## *The Fall*

**S**OMETHING THROBS AT THE BACK OF MY SKULL, DULL and insistent, pulling me up from the dark.

Flashes come back in pieces.

*The street. A scarred face. A voice low in my ear.*

*The sudden blackness.*

I open my eyes.

The room is half-dark, curtains drawn, the ceiling broken by restless shadows. A blanket covers me. The mattress beneath me is soft, molding to my body as though I belong here.

I don't.

My pulse spikes. I push the blanket aside, panic scraping raw against my throat. I'm still in my clothes. The white shirt and denim skirt are both intact, a little rumpled, still smelling faintly of coffee. Nothing has been taken from me but time.

Where am I?

The street. The dust.

Jace.

*A trap.*

My breath hitches as I force myself upright. My body aches, nerves buzzing from whatever he used.

*I can get through this.*

I see something shift in the corner of the strange room. And I freeze.

He's there, standing at the foot of the bed.

*Jace.*

Even the shadows can't hide him. His dark eyes are unblinking, and the scar cuts a brutal line across his face. His hair falls loose, framing a jaw too sharp, too merciless.

"You." My voice is nothing but a hoarse whisper, but it fills the silence like a scream. "How could you do this? HOW?"

His eyes flicker. Surprise? Regret? I don't know.

My hand closes around the nearest thing I can reach. It's a glass lamp on the bedside table. I yank the plug free.

And before I can think, it's flying through the air.

He moves fast, but not fast enough. The lamp shatters against the wall beside him, shards spraying out like stars. One cuts across his right side. Blood blooms red against his forearm.

He curses low under his breath, clutching the wound.

I don't wait. I run out the nearest exit I can see.

I find myself on the balcony, wrapped in the heavy night air.

Wind slaps at me, whipping my hair across my face. My chest heaves. I glance down. Endless city lights blur into dizzying streams of yellow and red.

It's too far, too high. If I jump, it's to my death.

Behind me, I hear footsteps.

He's coming.

I spin, throwing myself into a stance I've learned from Karate lessons our parents made me take since I was four. My body trembles, but I bare my teeth anyway.

"Get the fuck away from me, you bastard."

He doesn't answer. His eyes are unreadable, his steps deliberate, corralling me like prey.

I strike first. A kick to the midsection, enough to give me space to run past him. But he dodges it. His counter lands, palm to ribs, slamming the air from my lungs.

Pain cracks through me, and I stumble back.

The railing never catches me.

Only air. Only the plunge.

The world is a smear of black and neon and the howl of wind. I scream until my throat tears.

And then…

Impact. Not with the ground, but with him.

An arm locks around my waist, iron and heat. The rope bites above us, our single lifeline as the city spins below.

My scream dies into a gasp.

"Let me go," I choke out, but it's weak, almost pitiful.

"No." His voice is rough and harsh in my ear. "I can't."

I turn my head just enough to see his face.

The mask of shadows is gone. Only his eyes remain, burning and determined.

They're not the eyes of a monster. They're the eyes of a man bleeding.

A drop hits my cheek, warm and metallic.

*Blood.*

His blood. From the arm that holds the rope.

From the wound I gave him.

And still he holds.

We rise, inch by inch, until the railing meets us again. He shoves me over it. My legs shake as they find the solid surface of the balcony.

I want to run. But I don't.

He hauls himself after me, landing in a heap. His shirt is soaked, crimson smearing on his skin, his breath ragged.

We stare at each other, silence heavy as the night. He doesn't move. Doesn't reach for me. Just waits.

I could run. I should.

I kneel in front of him instead. "You're hurt."

His eyes flash in the shadows. "What are you doing?"

My handkerchief is already in my hands, trembling as I press it to his forearm. I knot it tight, clumsy but firm. Blood seeps through anyway. My throat aches. "That will help with the bleeding…for now."

When I look up, he's closer than I expected. Too close.

Heat radiates off him, his gaze steady, as steady as the first time I looked into those eyes.

I should hate him. He kidnapped me. He dragged me into this nightmare. But my pulse won't calm, not with his heat seeping into me, not with his eyes dragging me under like tides I can't fight.

His face is inches from mine. His hand brushes my jaw, his thumb grazing my skin like he has every right to. I should recoil. Instead, I shiver.

"Why?" I breathe.

"Because I can't stop," he says. "I can't let go."

Then his mouth claims mine.

The kiss is fire and steel, a clash of everything I should refuse and everything I can't resist. My hands curl into his shirt, pulling him closer, tasting blood and salt and him.

His tongue slides against mine, rough and starving, and I melt into him even as every nerve in me screams danger.

Everything else falls away—the city, the balcony, even the fear. My body betrays me completely, molding against his as though it's been waiting for this.

He drags me onto his lap, his thighs like iron beneath me, his chest hard and hot against mine. The cloth I tied around his forearm is already soaked, blood seeping warm through the fabric, but still his grip is unyielding. One hand digs in my hair, jerking my head back so he can take my mouth deeper, his tongue sliding hungrily against mine.

I moan into him. His other hand finds my hip, then my waist, then lower—gripping, squeezing, dragging me flush against him so I can feel every inch of his arousal pressing against the thin barrier of my skirt.

"Jace," I gasp against his lips, the word breaking.

"You feel that?" he growls, grinding me against him. "You do this to me, Lara. Every single time. That's why."

I shudder, my nails digging into his shoulders, my body rocking helplessly against his. Heat blooms everywhere, consuming and overwhelming.

I should fight. I should pull away. But instead I move with him, straddling him more firmly, my thighs opening over his lap as if my body's already chosen for me.

His hand slips beneath the hem of my skirt, fingers brushing the bare skin of my thigh. I gasp and jolt, but his grip on my hair keeps me right where he wants me.

"Say it," he demands, his breath burning against my mouth. "Say you want this."

"I… I shouldn't…"

"Say it." His fingers skim higher, knuckles grazing the damp fabric of my panties.

A strangled whimper escapes me. "I want you."

He curses harshly, then his mouth is on mine again. His hand presses harder against me through the thin cotton, rubbing slow circles that make my whole body arch into him. My hips grind helplessly against his, chasing the friction, and his groan rumbles through both of us like thunder.

"Goddamn it, Lara," he rasps, biting my lip hard enough to sting. "You'll destroy me."

I'm already destroyed. My body trembles, my thighs

shaking as he pushes me closer, closer, until the tension inside me snaps. Pleasure crashes through me, sharp and shattering, and I cry out against his mouth, my release spilling against his fingers.

He holds me through it, murmuring my name, his hand bruising on my hip. And even when the trembling subsides, he doesn't let go. He just pulls me tighter against him, grinding me against his hardness like he can't bear to stop.

I lean close, lips brushing his ear. "Let me give you this too."

His eyes widen, before he growls something low in his throat. His grip loosens just enough for me to slide down, my hand trailing over his chest, his abdomen, until I reach the hardness straining in his pants.

He hisses through his teeth as I palm him firmly, feeling the weight of him hot and pulsing in my hand. His head falls back against the railing, his jaw clenched, a raw sound tearing out of him.

"Lara…"

I stroke him through the fabric, slow at first, then harder, faster, watching him come apart under me. He grabs my wrist like he wants to stop me, but he doesn't. He can't. He's panting now, hips jerking into my hand, his body trembling with need.

I draw closer, mounting him until my hips are just above his thighs. Enough for him to feel that whatever he's feeling, I'm feeling it too.

"Let go, Jace," I whisper into the night. "Let go."

He swears, a guttural sound, before crushing his mouth to mine again. His kiss is frantic, teeth and tongue and desperation, even as his release builds under my hand. When I finally reach inside his waistband and wrap my fingers around him, hot and rigid and slick with need, he shudders violently.

"Fuck…" he groans against my mouth, thrusting into my fist, every muscle in his body drawn tight. I stroke him harder and harder, faster and faster, my other hand tangled in his hair, until he breaks.

His release spills hot across my hand, across his skin, and he buries his face in my neck with a hoarse cry, clutching me like I'm the only thing keeping him alive.

For a moment, it feels like I am.

When his breathing finally slows, when the tremors ease, he cups my face in his hand. I can feel the rope burns on his palm. His eyes are molten, tortured, and tender all at once. He kisses me softly this time, a contrast so sharp it hurts.

And I know…we are not done.

Not even close.

I know what he wants. I know what *I* want.

For one wild, terrifying second, I want him to take me right here, on the balcony, under the stars with the city lights watching.

I'm still shaking when he kisses me again, his chest heaving. His hands are trembling as they find my cheeks, blood from his wound slick and sticky against my skin.

"I don't want to run," I say against his mouth.

"If I keep you," he rasps brokenly, fiercely, "I destroy you."

The words should terrify me. Instead, they break me open.

Because even as he says it, he goes hard beneath me, throbbing against the soaked cotton of my panties, his body trembling with the effort to hold back.

I can't let him.

I kiss the corner of his mouth, tasting salt and blood and pain.

And I say the words.

"Then destroy me."

# CHAPTER 7

## The Dawn

**S**OMETHING INSIDE ME SNAPS.

I drag her against the cold concrete of the balcony, my hands rough, my body trembling with the kind of hunger I've buried since the moment I laid eyes on her.

The city is a blur below us, nothing but lights and noise. Here, it's only her. Her breath shudders into my mouth as I claim her lips, as if she's always been mine. I yank her skirt up, my hand pulling down the thin scrap of her soaked panties.

I stop for a moment. Not out of mercy, but because I feel her trembling, not just from fear.

I slide my fingers over her heat, testing and coaxing.

She's wet.

She's wet *for me.*

The realization nearly undoes me. So I do the only thing I could.

I lift her leg, nearly tearing her skirt in half, and bury my mouth in her. She tastes like cream, sweet and a little sticky, as my tongue lap at the juices from her earlier climax.

"Jace," she gasps, pulling at my hair with both hands, her hips jerking closer to my face.

I don't answer. Using my uninjured arm, I reach for her breasts under the cover of her shirt and bra, fingers stroking the nipples as my lips devour the soaking spot between her legs.

"I know, baby," I say against her thigh. "I know. You're ready for me."

"Jace," she says again, her knees bending over my shoulders as she writhes beneath me.

I slide up, covering her body with mine. It doesn't take long for me to lower the joggers, to free myself from the briefs completely. She moans as she pulls my shirt off, her teeth dragging across the bare skin of my chest, her hands digging into my arms, drawing more blood from the wound she'd given me.

And I'm above her, a breath away from making her completely mine.

"Tell me no, Lara," I rasp against her throat, my teeth scraping her skin. "I'll let you go. I promise."

One word could save her.

One word would save me.

"I won't," she says against my lips, then she drags her mouth to my scar, her tongue flicking out to trace it. "Never."

That single word breaks me. I push inside her, and the world explodes.

She gasps, her body so tight. Too tight.

My chest seizes when I realize.

She's untouched. Pure. I'm the first.

"Lara," I groan, my lips finding hers again. "God, you'll break me."

Her nails dig into my back, and I groan louder, half in agony, half in need. I can't stop. I move inside her, slow at first, then harder, deeper, claiming her in every way I know how.

She arches into me, tears glinting at the corners of her eyes, pain and pleasure tangled together.

"You'll destroy me, baby," I growl, kissing her hard, my hips driving her against the concrete until I feel it almost crack.

"Oh, god…Jace!" Her voice breaks on my name. "Don't stop. Please, don't stop—"

Her plea undoes whatever control I had left. I take her brutally, but my hand cradles her face, my mouth drinks every cry she makes. I move faster and faster, until I feel her clench around me, her scream muffled against my lips.

I spill into her with a ragged, broken cry, every drop of me claiming her. I clutch her as if letting go means death.

For one blistering moment, we're one. Flesh and soul and shadow.

When it ends, I collapse against her, our sweat and my blood between us.

Her scent clings to me. Her heartbeat thunders against

my chest, wild and alive. And in that moment, I know the truth I've fought to deny since the beginning.

I love her.

God help me, I love her.

"I should never have touched you," I say, pressing my lips to her soaked hair.

Her hand cups my jaw, her eyes steady despite what I've made of her. "But you did. And I'll never regret it."

I kiss her once more. It's soft and reverent, because it's the last time I'll ever be allowed to. Then I pull away, the shadows closing back around me like a noose.

"Your bag's in the closet. Take my jacket if you want to."

She stares at me. "What are you talking about?"

I don't answer at first. Even as I stand before her bleeding, heart torn open, I help her back into her clothes. I put my arms around her waist and pull her up. I press my lips to her forehead, running my hand through her hair.

I know. I'll never get to touch her like this again.

"Run, Lara," I say softly. "This is the last mercy I have left."

She doesn't move.

"Jace…"

I turn away. "I promised I'll let you go."

Then I walk into the room and sit on the same chair at the foot of the bed.

She stumbles in after me, still wobbly on her feet. It doesn't take long for her to find her things. She slides my jacket on, the fabric swallowing her smaller frame.

She looks at me for the last time, reaching for the doorknob.

"I don't know what to say," she says, her voice small.

I smile at her. "You never had to say anything. Goodbye, Lara."

She doesn't answer.

In a breath, she's gone. Her hair loose, her skirt torn, my blood still drying on her skin.

I watch her from the balcony.

She reaches the street without incident, and mercifully manages to hail a taxi.

I should feel empty. Instead, I feel alive for the first time in years.

"Lara," I whisper into the night, her name torn out of me like prayer.

Like damnation.

I could chase her. I could take her back. I could burn the world down and keep her. I could wage war and win against impossible odds.

I could do it all for her.

But I don't.

Because if I love her at all, I have to let her go.

So I sink into the shadows again, bloodied and haunted, with nothing left but the taste of her on my lips and the fire she's branded into my heart.

And I wait for dawn to come.

# BRUISE-COLORED LOVE

# CHAPTER 1

## *The Temptation*

I SWEAR I WILL NEVER FALL FOR SOMEONE LIKE HIM.

I repeat it every morning like prayer, or superstition. Or a spell I can clench between my teeth so I don't swallow it by accident.

And then he leans in the doorway of the student council room, one cheek bruised, mouth cut at the corner, smirk set to devastation levels, and my pulse does the exact opposite of prayer.

It races.

And it gives in to temptation.

The silence between heartbeats opens—small and bright, a beautiful and dangerous trap—and I walk into it.

"Move," I say, arms full of folders, hair pinned into the version of me adults trust.

"What's the magic word, princess?" he asks, not budging an inch.

"Please don't make me staple your mouth shut before the outreach drive," I say. "I need both hands to collect all the donations I could."

He lifts both palms, laughing. "Donations. Be still, my heart."

"It would be a public service to the inner city villages." I shoulder past him and place the folders on the table with a resounding *thunk*. "Did you finish painting the backdrop?"

"Two coats," he says. "Three if you count the one on my lungs."

"You're not supposed to paint in a closed room."

"You're not supposed to micromanage a guy who volunteered on his day off." He leans into my space, that lazy grin I hate, the citrus-ash scent I hate more. "But here we are."

"Here we are," I echo, rolling my eyes.

Outside, the auditorium speakers hiccup with feedback. Inside, the room's fan ticks like a tired metronome. I circle items on the checklist so hard the pen almost tears the paper.

He watches me. He always watches me, as if I'm a language he only half understands but wants to speak without an accent.

"Tell me again why you're here," I say. "And don't even try to lie."

"Because the guidance counselor said 'service hours,'" he says. "And because you asked nicely."

"I didn't ask," I lie.

I did ask for him. Not by name, but by skill.

I knew he was the only one who could paint the backdrop for the fundraiser show without batting an eye.

He tips his head. "You didn't have to. Who else could put up with me?"

I hate the way that lands. I hate the way my chest answers with a soft, traitorous ache.

"Do you ever," I ask, still looking at my checklist, "get tired of being a problem?"

"Do you ever," he fires back, "get tired of putting up with problems that can't be solved?"

We hold each other's eyes like that. Whatever is between us feels it's stretched too tight.

Around us, the room hums and thrums. The hallway fills and empties with bodies and noise. Between us, the unsaid is a knife we both press a little too close to our throats.

Then I clear mine. "If the backdrop peels, I'll personally haunt you."

"Hot," he says, and saunters out before I can scold him for existing.

I look at the space where he stood a second too long, and turn away.

He shows up again two nights later at the university gates, leaning against the hood of his gray car, jaw blooming purple, knuckles skinned almost raw.

"What happened?" The words slip out before I can stop them. "Didn't see you in class yesterday."

"What do you think?" he says, grinning.

"You're such an idiot."

"And you're such a saint. Wanna heal me?"

"I don't fix broken things," I say automatically.

But my hand is already reaching up, thumb hovering over the bruise. I'm close enough to see the flecks of gold in his otherwise dark brown eyes. Close enough to see the new crack in his bottom lip where the skin should be soft.

He catches my wrist and holds it there. Not hard, but just enough to make my pulse jump against his fingers.

"See?" he rasps. "You already do."

"Let go," I say.

He does. Immediately. The way he obeys makes my stomach drop. I hate him more for that than for the smirk.

"Get in," he says, tilting his chin at the passenger door.

"Now?"

"Unless you're busy scheduling your next attempt at saving the world. You should try living normally like the rest of us, princess. Who knows, you might like it."

I frown at him, ready to bite back.

But I hesitate.

The look in his eyes says everything his lips couldn't.

*Try.*

*Stay.*

I should say no. Mama is waiting with dinner. I have a speech to polish for the next district outreach, our biggest with a dozen *barangay* involved.

But the car door is already open. The night smells like rain waiting for permission to fall.

"Fifteen minutes," I say.

He smiles like I said forever.

We drive aimlessly through the early evening traffic.

Windows down. Air thick with the coming storm.

"Why do you fight so much?" I ask.

"Because it feels like proof," he says. "Like if I hit hard enough, the world will hit back and at least then I'll know it sees me."

"That's the stupidest thing I've ever heard."

"Yeah?" He glances at me. "Why do you work so much?"

"Because it feels like protection," I say before I can edit it. "If I have a plan, then at least the world has to argue with me in bullet points. I'm prepared for it."

He laughs. "Wow. Look at us. Two completely different coping mechanisms. One disaster."

"Speak for yourself."

"Princess," he says, almost fondly. "You are the most beautiful disaster I've ever seen."

I look out at the city streets. *Sari-sari* stores lit like tiny altars, people ducking into tricycles with plastic bags looped over hair, a kid in a Superman shirt hopping over potholes like lava.

"Pull over," I say.

He does, under a flickering streetlamp that buzzes like an insect with secrets.

We sit in the loud quiet of a car cooling down. His breath is rough. Mine is worse.

"Don't," I say.

"I didn't do anything."

"You're about to."

He chuckles, then sobers almost immediately. "I'm really not good for you."

"Tell me something I don't know."

"And you're the best thing that's happened to me in a long time."

"I know that, too," I say, and the honesty hurts more than the bruise on his face.

We look at each other until the light from the streetlamp steadies and the shadows fall.

Then he kisses me.

It's always the same first second. It's like falling into a well I watched him dig.

The second after that is different every time. This one tastes like the coming storm. This one tastes like apologies we will not say. This one tastes like the mouth you only have when you think you're about to be forgiven for what you could never be.

His hand cups my jaw. My fingers knot in the collar of his shirt. He pulls me closer, a little too hard. I let him. I kiss him back, a little harder.

When we pull apart, my breath shivers.

"You can't keep doing this," I tell him, still panting a little.

"Doing what?"

"Picking fights. Getting hurt. Dragging me into your mess."

He huffs a laugh that isn't funny. "Dragging you in? You dive, babe."

"Don't call me 'babe.'"

"What should I call you then?"

"Nothing," I say, voice sharp. "Or my name. Or President, if you want to be annoying. Annoying I can deal with."

"President it is." He leans in again, close enough that I can see the pulse leap at his throat. "You're shaking."

"Because you make me so mad."

"That's not why."

"Maybe it is."

"Maybe," he says, because he knows when not to push. He pulls back, puts the car in gear, drives me home.

At my curb he doesn't say goodnight. I don't say stay. We never do.

When I get to my room, I press my palm to the middle of my chest.

I count.

*Beat. Beat.*

Then silence.

That pause fills with his name, with the shape of his smile, with the stupid tilt of his head. I tell myself it's just adrenaline.

I tell myself it's not love. I tell myself the bruise blooming on my mouth is blotted lipstick.

I tell myself to sleep.

I tell myself to stop.

# CHAPTER 2



OUR OUTREACH DRIVE HUMS LIKE A MACHINE I BUILT from stubbornness.

People line up. Kids grab bread with both hands and run away laughing. The seniors get their blood pressure taken and tell me stories I didn't ask for but need.

He is there, hauling boxes like they're lighter in his hands than they really are. Sweat slicks the hair at his neck. Volunteers orbit him—half wary, half drawn.

I hate that watching him makes my teeth ache.

When it starts to drizzle, he looks up at the sky like an old friend and grins.

I feel it tug painfully at the inside of my stomach.

"Great job, President," he says later, hoisting the last crate into the van.

"Thank you," I say to the van, because if I look at him he'll know what I really mean.

He waits. He's patient in the exact ways that hurt me.

"You coming to the concert after?" he asks. "Your beloved cultural hour?"

"It's not an hour," I say. "But yes. A lot of alumni will be there."

"Save me a seat?"

"You never sit," I say, smiling without meaning to. "You lurk."

"Then save me a place to lurk."

"I don't reserve corners."

"For me you always do," he says. "Even if you won't admit it."

It's too close to the truth, and I hate him for it.

Instead of raising funds, the cultural concert raises chaos like Murphy's Law.

Lights misbehave. A microphone squeaks and refuses to work since. One of the performers is running late from a traffic accident across town.

My vice president whispers that the head of the alumni association is here, which means we have to look like we know what we're doing if we want the funds to expand the College of Management library.

He appears in the wings like a problem I forgot to solve.

He lurks, as always.

"You look like a headline," he says, taking in my suit, my too-sleek hair, my pale face and my trembling hands. "All caps."

"And you look like a bad idea," I say. "In italics. Ripped jeans? Really?"

He laughs. "You're funny when you're stressed."

"I'm funny when you're around," I snap. "It's a symptom."

"Of what?"

"Poor judgment."

"On a scale of one to disaster," he murmurs, leaning in, "how bad is it tonight?"

I nearly tell him it's catastrophic, but I really want to say: *Old habit, new bruise.*

Instead I say, "Get back to your corner. Keep lurking. You're good at it."

He salutes, backs away, but his eyes snag on the soloist walking past, Alton from the debate club, a perfectly decent boy who sometimes carries my laptop after team meetings.

Alton nods at me, friendly. "Good luck, Bea. Break a leg. Or whatever presidents do."

I smile. "Thanks."

"Who's that?" he asks after Alton passes, voice suddenly flat.

"Don't start."

"I asked you a question."

"You're not my boyfriend."

"That's convenient," he says, mouth tight.

"For both of us," I say. "Focus, please. There are donors and alumni present. Try not to fight anyone tonight. *Please.*"

He snorts, but his eyes are still on Alton. I feel the heat of something ugly unfurl from him.

The performances start with a traditional *rondalla*. The lights go up. The city outside exhales rain against the roof.

We almost make it through the first half of the show.

Between acts, Alton jokes with a technician about the old, wobbly microphone stand and casually claps my shoulder as he passes. I feel the weight of his stare like a hand around my throat.

"Hey," he says, stepping in front of Alton. "Watch your hands."

Alton blinks at him in confusion. "What?"

"I saw you," he says. "Hands. Shoulder. Watch it."

"Are you serious, bro?" Alton laughs, looking to me for help.

"Backstage isn't the place," I say, stepping between them. "Please. Both of you."

Alton lifts both palms and backs away, irritation written clean across his face.

He steps closer. "You let him touch you?"

"He didn't touch me," I hiss. "He's my teammate. This is my event. You don't get to be a scene in it."

Something flickers in his eyes.

Hurt, maybe. Fast as lightning, then gone just as quickly.

"You never pick me," he says quietly.

It's the truest thing he's ever said.

"I pick what needs me," I retort.

And it's the truest thing I've ever said.

He flinches like I swung a bat and it smacked him right across the face.

He doesn't say or do anything for a few long seconds. Then he takes a deep breath.

"I'm going." The words leave his mouth like the rain outside the auditorium.

He disappears before I can decide whether to follow or not.

I run the rest of the show on autopilot. My brain is a list, but my chest is a wound.

When it's over, when the alumni shake my hand and say words like *promise* and *potential* and *allocations*, I smile like the kind of girl who never chooses wrong. I go to the parking lot and breathe dark air that smells like wet asphalt and exhaustion.

He is there, of course, smoking a cigarette, sitting on the hood of his car that still bears traces of the downpour.

"Congrats, President," he mutters.

"I told you not to start something. You promised me one night without drama."

"I didn't promise anything," he says. "I don't know how."

"You made me a liar," I say. "You made me choose

between my job and you and you're mad I didn't pick you in the middle of a live show."

He laughs humorlessly, then rubs a hand over his face, cigarette between fingers. "I didn't make you do anything. You never let me make you do anything."

"So what is this?" I demand, pain blooming into anger. "What do you want from me? A schedule? A curfew? A leash?"

He takes a step closer.

Then grabs my wrist.

It's not hard. It's not gentle either.

But it's enough to leave the ghost of his fingers on my skin tomorrow morning.

"Don't ever talk about leashes to me," he says, voice dangerously low "You have no idea what it's like to be…to be—"

"Owned?" I say, because I know about his father and the belt and the way he learned to take pain without moving. "I know. That's why I'm still here."

"Then be here," he begs. "Like now. Pick me now. Bea, please."

"I can't pick you when you're like this, Mike! How could I?"

"When I'm like what?

"When you're hurting yourself by trying to hurt someone else first."

He lets go like my skin burned him. He turns and

punches the concrete wall. The sound is like a crack of thunder. He bites back a swear word and a groan.

"Great," I say numbly. "Now you're bleeding."

"Don't," he says. "Don't pity me. Don't fix me. Just don't."

"Then what do you want?"

He looks at me then. His face is stone, but his eyes are filled with the fire of terror.

"I want you to love me when I'm not easy. Because that's the only version of me I know how to be."

I take a step back, inwardly flailing.

Then I hear it.

My heart thundering right back.

A beat. A pulse. Another.

The space between them fills with all the things I could say and don't.

"I do," I whisper. "That's the problem."

We stand inside the fallout of that confession.

"Come with me," he says suddenly. "Just for tonight. We'll drive nowhere. We'll get the best *inasal* for dinner with what's left of my money. We can be bad at this together and maybe that makes it good."

"I have to lock up," I say. "I have to sign forms for the equipment. I have to—"

"You always 'have to,'" he says, the words breaking. "You always put me after the list."

"And you always ask me to be the kind of girl who doesn't keep promises."

He laughs once, the sound bitter and ugly. "So we're done."

"I didn't say that."

"You didn't have to."

He gets in his car and leaves rubber and the threat of tears on the wet pavement.

I press my hand to my chest and count.

*Beat. Beat.*

Then silence.

But I can hear it howl.

# CHAPTER 3

## *The Forest*

**F**OR TWO DAYS, HE DOESN'T TEXT.

I sleep badly and do my job too well and pretend I don't look up every time a gray car rumbles past the university gate. I walk through my classes like a zombie on crack. I even ace a surprise exam.

But I still hear the howling in my emptiness.

On the third night, he calls just before the clock strikes twelve.

"Hey," he says, voice hoarse. "I'm at the court. The one near the river."

"It's midnight," I answer automatically, a little breathless.

"I know."

"What do you need?"

He chuckles softly. "You."

I sit down on the floor next to my bed before my knees give out. "Is your father—"

"Not tonight. Just…come?"

I go. I don't tell anyone. I throw a jacket over my plain shirt and cotton pants, and tie my hair and run.

The ride-share man doesn't ask any questions. He only plays Bee Gees songs on his stereo as he drives, careful not to catch my eye.

He's sitting cross-legged at center court, hood up, shoulders hunched. The court lights paint him in faint silver.

I sit beside him without a word.

"You always come," he says, not looking at me.

"That's not true."

"Don't lie to me on my favorite court. Especially not tonight."

I rest my head on his shoulder. He lets me. His breath shakes a little.

"I'm sorry," he whispers into the dark. "About the show. About Alton. About everything."

"Stop apologizing for everything," I say. "Pick one thing and be specific."

He huffs out a small laugh. "I'm sorry I grabbed your wrist."

"Thank you," I say. "I'm sorry I made you feel like my job matters more than you."

"It should," he says. "It's the version of you that makes sense. It's what makes you…you, I guess."

"I want the version that loves you to make sense too."

He turns his face into my hair, gently pulling off the rubber band from my ponytail. "Me too."

We sit there, bodies leaning like battered trees in the same storm. The river hums to itself behind the court. A dog barks twice, then decides to give us peace and quiet.

"Do you think we can do this?" he asks. "Like people do? Not like a movie, or a disaster? Just…dates and fights that don't end in bleeding and broken things. And maybe one day I show up to a concert and clap like a normal person. I may decide not to lurk anymore. What do you think?"

"I don't know," I answer honestly. "But I want to try."

"Okay," he says. "Then let's try."

For one fragile moment, it feels as if we built a bridge out of the worst of us.

It feels as if the world might just let us cross.

For once.

Trying lasts exactly eight days.

For eight days he texts before he shows up. He stops smoking, then starts again, then stops. He puts ice on his knuckles instead of punching anything. He comes to dinner at our house and tells my mother about the houses he wants to build for people who don't get houses. My mother smiles at him with soft eyes I have never seen her use on a boy.

On the ninth day he is late to my intercollegiate debate

final and I am okay. On the tenth he is even later to my presentation to the alumni association—and I am not.

On the eleventh day he does not come at all.

He calls at midnight.

He is crying and drunk and at the court again, and the old anger and the old tenderness tear my ribcage in half.

"I needed you there," I say, voice flat and tight with trying not to sob. "For once, I needed you."

"I'm sorry," he says. "I got into it with—" He stops. "I messed up. Again. I don't know why I keep choosing wrong."

"You do," I say, and the cruelty surprises me. "Because it's the only way you know you're still…you."

Silence. The kind that lands with heavy finality.

Then he says, in a small, almost childlike voice, "Don't leave."

"I'm not," I answer quietly. "I'm finally staying with myself."

He makes a noise like a boy broken in half. "Please, Bea. Please."

"I love you," I say. It sounds like it's both mercy and pain.

"I love you so much it's destroying me," I continue. "At times…I even want it to."

"Then let it," he says, with sudden fierceness. "Let it destroy you. Let it destroy both of us."

"I can't, Mike. I can't."

There it is.

The choice that has been waiting like a wolf at the edge of the dark forest.

I listen to him breathe. Maybe for the last time.

"Okay," he says after what seems like forever. "Okay."

We hang up.

I press my hand to my chest and count.

*Beat. Beat.*

Silence.

In it, I feel something close. Not the love. Not the want.

The door that lets me live.

# CHAPTER 4

## The Bridge

**W**E MEET ONE LAST TIME, BECAUSE ENDINGS DESERVE daylight.

At the footbridge over the *estero* near the university, the early morning sun glinting off water that pretends to be clean, he leans against the rail wearing the same dark hoodie from the court, hair a mess, eyes milked out from not sleeping.

"You look like hell," I say, because love has always been cruelty wrapped in care.

"You look like the truth," he says, because he always returns it with something I don't know where to put.

People move around us, caught in their own little worlds.

A woman in scrubs, a man holding a cake like it's a baby,

a teenager in a school uniform practicing a speech under his breath.

"We're not good," I tell him honestly.

"We could be," he says.

I hear the hope he knows better than to feed.

But it's too late for that kind of thing now.

"I don't mean ever," I say. "I mean right now. This version."

He nods, hands jammed into the pockets of his ripped jeans. "I know."

"Say the thing," I ask softly. "The honest version."

He sighs. "I don't know how to love you without making you smaller than the thing I'm trying to survive."

I swallow hard at that.

"And I don't know how to love you," I answer, "without trying to turn you into the kind of person I can take to a donor dinner."

He laughs, but the sound shatters softly midway. "God. We're really bad at this."

"Not always," I say, smiling because it's true. "Sometimes we were perfect."

He nods. "The car. The court. Even the rain."

"The dinner," I add. "The almost."

"The almost," he echoes.

We stand there, two people who did not manage to keep the bridge from collapsing.

But we know—there really was a bridge. Even if it wasn't meant to last.

"Can I ask one more thing?" he says.

I nod. "Just one."

Because I know boundaries are pieces of love dressed in armor.

"Kiss me," he says.

The way he says it is not a demand. It's a prayer.

I step close. I cup his face, careful of old bruises and fresh cracks, gentle to the point of cruelty. I kiss him slowly, almost dreamily—mouth soft, breath slow, the shape of us simple for once.

It's the kind of kiss you give to broken things.

His hands stay at his sides, but I feel him tremble.

When I pull back we both laugh, not because it's funny but because surviving it is.

"Thank you," he says.

"Don't thank me," I say. "Just…take care."

He nods.

He will try.

I will try.

We will both fail and then try again for people who are not each other.

I nod back, feeling the tears sloshing behind my lids.

I walk away first. I don't look back.

At the far end of the bridge, I press two fingers to my wrist and count.

*Beat. Beat.*

Then silence.

In that pause, he lives.

Not as a wound. Not as a man I'm waiting on. But as a color under the skin, fading and permanent at once. As proof that I loved like the worst and best parts of me learned at the same time.

A bruise-colored love.

I still remember him that way.

In the silence between heartbeats, he stays.

Where the ache is honest, where the lesson is clean, where I am whole enough to choose the next person with both hands.

Where I know I will not be destroyed from that love.

But I never forget.

# THE
# HOTEL
# ROOM

# CHAPTER 1

## *The Twilight*

**T**HERE HE IS.

I don't expect him to be there when I open the door.

But he proves me wrong.

I don't ask why he chooses to meet in the same hotel I do. Maybe it's coincidence. Maybe it's fate, or maybe fate is just another word for good timing but with all the wrong reasons.

He leans against the doorframe as if he belongs to the twilight, all shadows and half-hooded eyelids. He smells like cigarette smoke, wearing the same dark blue jacket from years ago.

He doesn't look at me right away.

And I remember the first time I saw him, all those years ago. I was his supervisor at the insurance company and he'd been an encoder. He'd been the fastest to meet quotas in my team, but he never said much to anyone. After a month, he started waiting for me to finish work, then waited until I got into my taxi. He even asked me to text him once I reached home.

Months later, he got into the taxi with me. I took him to a motel.

Then I moved to a government office in Manila.

"You're late," I tell him.

"You aren't supposed to be here," he replies, finally meeting my eyes. "What will they say about their golden girl sneaking around?"

I shake my head, a little tiredly. "And yet here we are."

"Here we are," he echoes, giving me a smile.

It's lopsided, weary, familiar. God, it's familiar.

It's always like this with us. Half-smiles. Half-truths. Half-promises. All of them crumbling at the edges.

The door clicks shut behind him. The rain outside is a distant hush against the windowpane. He shrugs off his damp jacket, tosses it onto the armchair like he owns the room, like he owns this silence between us. But he doesn't. He never did.

The room is quiet except for the hum of the city below. Floor-to-ceiling windows show a skyline we both once dreamed of conquering.

"This is a big change," he says softly, leaning against the

wall, watching me, his eyes tracing every movement like he hasn't forgotten a thing. "The room's clean, for a start. Surprised you said you're going to foot the bill. My baby girl can afford better now, can't she? "

I scowl at him. I got the room at a discount using the Undersecretary's name, but I don't want to give him the satisfaction of being right.

"Don't call me that," I bite out instead. "I'm not your baby. And I'm definitely not a girl."

He frowns down at me. "You'll always be to me, Lee."

I shake my head, then sit at the table and pour a glass of red wine.

"Fancy," he murmurs.

I incline my head in casual agreement, as if I didn't book this hotel because of him. As if we didn't always end up together, somehow, when the world got too complicated and we ran out of excuses not to forget.

At least for a while.

He doesn't ask for a drink, but I pour for him too. Old habits, I guess.

We used to drink light beer and eat fried chicken, after the motel.

"I thought you would appreciate something…different," I say.

He smiles.

But I know he doesn't do different. He'd self-destructed weeks after I left my old workplace. By the time I'd heard about it from practically everyone at the insurance company, I was already far away from Iloilo.

"How long are you gonna be in town for?" he asks, sliding into the seat across mine. The soft light of the room cast half his face in eerie, distorted shadow.

"Just the night," I answer. "I'm flying back to work tomorrow evening. I told my boss I'm visiting my parents."

He lifts his glass to me in a mock toast. "Clever girl."

I don't answer, choosing instead to let the word go. I take a sip of my wine, not looking at him but at the bed before us.

"So why now?" he asks softly. "Why this room, this night?"

I sigh. "I know what happened. What you did when I left. You shouldn't have done that."

"What did I do?" he challenges me, almost immediately.

"You didn't listen to anyone. You completely and utterly disregarded all authority by nearly killing Doc Simeon. You're lucky they didn't have you arrested."

He slams the glass down, wine sloshing all over the polished wood. Then he jumps to his feet.

"I didn't come here for this bullshit," he says. "I came for you."

In the dim light, I can see his shoulders shaking, but his voice sounds steady.

"I know," I answer softly.

I put my own glass down and stand, blocking his way.

"That's why I'm here. I want to ask you to stop whatever it is you're doing before you can't anymore."

He shakes his head. "I can't, Lee. You know I can't."

"Dennis." His name escapes my lips, an apology he never asked for. An apology I could never say out loud.

He winces at the sound—and there it is.

That knife-twist in my chest. The one I thought I'd buried under logic and time.

The familiar, breathless tightness whenever I look into his deep-set eyes, so dark they're almost black.

I miss him.

"I love you, Lee," he says. "I loved you the moment you told the VP you could put me to work. You never judged. You just believed."

The pain reaches my stomach, making me feel deathly cold.

*Love.*

He still loves me.

But I don't say it back.

"I still believe," I say cautiously. "And I never judged you. I knew you were better than everyone else, even if you didn't finish college. I never looked at what you had on paper."

He freezes, his body wound tight like a rubber band ready to snap.

"I looked at you," I continue. "I still see you. I still see the man who promised me he won't let me down."

"I promised you," he retorts icily. "I didn't promise any of them. When Simeon questioned my work, I told him to fuck off and retire. He shouted at me, made everyone hear that I was a dropout who couldn't even meet quota. So I broke his nose. People forget I used to be good at Silat."

I sigh impatiently. "Christ."

"It was never the same without you, baby girl," he says, softer now. "It all got fucked up so quickly. I didn't even realize I was already fired. I was just too…mad."

"At me," I offer.

He shakes his head. "No. At the world. At them. Never at you."

That does it.

I put my arms around him. His heartbeat thunders in my ear.

"Don't go then," I say. "Stay. Stay the night."

"Say it then," he mutters into my hair. "Just say it, Lee."

I take a deep breath.

"I love you, Dennis." And I just couldn't stop there. "I miss you. It's not the same without you."

He doesn't answer right away. He doesn't even move an inch.

"You should have just told me the minute I walked through that door," he finally says. His eyes take me in, up and down, lips to throat, chest to forehead.

I shake my head and step back, but he reaches for me, hands sliding around my waist.

"I wanted to make sure you're still not completely insane," I shoot back. "I heard stories. Not so flattering ones, I'm afraid."

He laughs then. That low, familiar sound that vibrates through me like a memory I could never shake.

I sit on the edge of the bed. He joins me a beat later.

We're not touching, but the space between us is electric.

"So," I say, "do you want to talk about it?"

He doesn't say anything in response. He just looks at me like he's memorizing every inch of me all over again. I can see it in his eyes.

"Do you remember the first time?" he asks instead.

"The motel in Molo? Or us?"

"Both."

I close my eyes. I remember the rain. I stayed back at the office to sign hundreds of new membership cards. I remember the feel of his hand around mine as he slid into the taxi next to me.

The way he asked me, "Do you want to forget everything for a while?"

It felt like a lifetime ago.

"You made me feel like flying," I say, smiling a bit.

Now, he touches my hand, lightly. "You said you didn't believe in forever. You said you believe in seizing the moment."

"And you said you didn't believe in anything at all."

We both lie sometimes.

He doesn't answer. Not with words.

He moves closer. His hands slide into my hair, and mine find his chest.

"Tell me to stop, Lee," he breathes.

"I can't."

And I don't.

The clothes come off in pieces, peeling away the years between us. Our touches feel like confessions we could never say.

It's like no time has passed at all. His hands know the slope of my hips. My mouth remembers the taste of his name. We fall back into each other like drowning people finding air.

The night is slow, lingering, beautiful. We spend it tangled in the thick white sheets. Fingers skimming skin. Kisses that ask questions, ones answered only in gasps and caresses.

When he whispers my name, tells me he missed *us*, I wonder if he feels it too—the pain of something lost and almost found again.

We don't promise anything.

But we say *I love you*.

Because in this hotel room, that is the most real thing in the world.

# CHAPTER 2

*The Mark*

**W**E DON'T SLEEP.

Morning comes quietly. The light is gentle as it skims over my skin, filtering in small ripples through the blinds.

He holds me close and says, "This doesn't change anything."

"I know," I answer. "At least I tried."

But we both feel it. That thing in the air. That almost that always threatens to become more, if only we let it.

He kisses me squarely on the mouth.

"I think that's why I love you," he murmurs against my lips. "And that's why you'll leave."

A lone tear slides down my cheek. He brushes it away with the back of his hand, exhaling softly.

"Promise me you'll do better," I tell him. "Just try. Not for me. For you. You deserve more than what you're doing to yourself."

He pulls me closer, his fingers running through my hair.

"I already had more," he says. "I had you."

The dam finally breaks.

I spend the sunrise crying in his arms.

He doesn't say anything. He just keeps holding me, soothing my tears with soft kisses and feather-light touches.

The last thing I remember is seeing his skinned knuckles, his callused palms, as his fingers trace the gentlest lines down my cheeks.

"Goodbye, Dennis," I say softly, dreamily, before drifting off to an exhausted sleep.

The room is bright when I wake up.

I check the time on my phone, then stare at the ceiling. I know before I look around the room.

He's gone.

A note sits on the nightstand in his handwriting.

Still blocky, a little too sharp. Just like him.

*Thank you for the night. You'll always be my baby girl.*

I trace the words, the same way I traced the hard, sullen lines of his face.

# THE HOTEL ROOM

And in the quiet between heartbeats, in the space where the tears and the ache should be, I realize something.

We never made promises.

But love doesn't need those to leave a mark.

It just needs one night.

# ABOUT THE AUTHOR

Shirley Siaton writes edgy and evocative novels and poems. Her worlds are in a deliciously dark cross-section of the romance, neo-noir, action, contemporary, and fantasy genres. Her background in various Asian martial arts inspires a lot of her work.

She has several books of fiction and poetry released since February 2023. Her first book is the free verse collection *Black Cat and other poems. Befallen* (March 2025) is her first full-length novel. She also pens juvenile literature as Shirley Parabia.

She is an award-winning writer, poet, and journalist in English, Filipino, and Hiligaynon. Her essays, short stories, and poems have been published internationally in print and digital media. Her multi-lingual plays have been staged in the Philippines.

Shirley is a black belt in Shotokan Karate and an international certified fitness coach. She has a Master's degree in Public Administration and works in education, wellness, and publishing. Originally from Iloilo City, she lives in the Middle East with her husband and two daughters.

# ON THE WEB

*Shirley's official website:*
**shirleysiaton.com**

*Complete reading guide:*
**shirley.pub**

*Subscribe to Shirley's VIP list for free exclusive updates:*
**newsletter.shirleysiaton.com**